"Someday," Naty repeats, yawning.
But for now
it is time to go home
and dream pony dreams
all night long.

Then all the musicians
and the dancers
and the floats
and the oxen
and the ponies
and the puppets
(except for Naty)
march to another part of town.
Naty says, "Someday I'll be big
enough to march away with them."
"Someday," says Papa.
The music fades away.

Naty wants a hotcake with strawberry jam.
That's her favorite.

There are so many different kinds of treats.

Boys shoo bees off piles of candies. The Cake Lady shimmies to the marimba boys' mambo. Women sell fried grasshoppers— they really do.

"Oh, yes! Can we do it again?"

"*Claro.*" He laughs. "Of course. Every year. Now, you must be hungry. What does my favorite mouse want to eat?"

Then the costume lifts off her.
The air feels so good.
"There, Naty." It's Papa! "Did you have fun?"

Puppets are bumping and jumping. Ponies are twirling.
Games and church bells are ringing. Naty blows on her whistle.
"Papa, where are you?" But no one can hear.

At last, they come to the square. People shout and clap and
cheer. The way they do year after year.

But where is Papa?

The square is filled with laughing and lights. The dragon
ride goes up-up-up. The girls scream.

The pony boys are prancing ahead.

She has found the parade!

Naty starts to spin . . . Then she thinks, "I'd better not."

All the ponies are dark except the one in the middle. Its rider wears silver buckles down his legs. He looks so proud.

"Someday," Naty thinks, "I will wear silver buckles and ride the white pony. But now I am happy. I, the dancing mouse, have found the parade."

And now Naty hears:
Boomf-boomf-boomf!
It's Oscar's drum!
And is that popcorn she smells?
Yes, it's *palomitas*, all right.
She turns a corner and *"¡Mira!"*
she shouts. "Look!"

Then she sees the shop where they make the *piñatas*. And the
Frog Burger sign. And there is the shop where they cut Papa's hair.
¡Sí, sí, sí! Yes, yes, yes!
First turn right and then turn left.

Now it is dark.

Down alleys she goes, chasing shadows and sounds. There are doors in the sky and stars on the ground.

Just when Naty wants to cry, she says, "I know, I *know* I can find my way!"

But Naty shouts, "I'm the biggest mouse in the valley!" and she blows her whistle.

"*¡Adios, gatos!* Go away!"

Night is coming. Out of the shadows come snaky tails and green eyes. Many cats are lurking. They look hungry.

She follows the music to a door. But it's only a radio. Inside, an old man is fixing shoes.

"Where is the parade, señor?"

"Wait just a minute. Don't you want your boots shined?" he asks.

"No time," Naty says. "I've got to hurry. Besides, they're new!"

As she runs along, there's a tug on her tail. A dog
wants to play.

"No, no, *perro*! Let go, let go! I must find the parade!"

On the corner, an old woman is making tortillas. Naty asks,
"Where is the parade, *abuela*?"

But the old woman says, "Wait—you must be a hungry
mouse." She offers her a piece of cheese.

"No, *gracias*," says Naty. "I'm in a hurry." And off she goes.

¡Ay, caramba! She's lost!
The music is bouncing off walls and calling her
from alleyways, but she cannot find the parade.

Naty marches with the puppet people, tall as streetlights. They dance and spin and bump into each other. "I'm the only dancing mouse in the parade!" Naty sings.

She has practiced all year to dance like a mouse. She wants to spin faster than anyone else— around and around until her feet leave the ground. As fast as a spider she spins and dances and spins and spins until she's so dizzy she almost falls over.

Her little clay whistle goes clattering away. Naty spins down an alley to find it. There it is—she gives it a tweet.

But then she sees . . .

Papa helps Naty put on her costume. He gives her a present, a little bird whistle that fits in her pocket. "Now go wait with the puppet people," he tells her. "Be a good mouse, Naty, and I'll be there to meet you at the end of the parade."

The music starts calling people from all over town and the roof dogs start barking.

The trumpets go *ta-ta-ta!*

Old José plays his fiddle. *Zing-zing-zing!*

And Naty's friend Oscar bangs a big drum. *Boomf-boomf-boomf*, it goes—just like Naty's heart.

The *piña* girls have come from the north to do the Pineapple Dance.
And sunflower girls from the south smile like butterflies.

Then comes El Pescado—the Dance of the Fish. The fish-men
throw nets to catch the crowd, and everyone laughs like silvery
minnows.

All day long, the town fills up with happy strangers.
Naty and her papa follow the crowd to where the parade
will begin. There are oxen in the streets with wet noses
and rings in them big as bracelets.

"This one did. Some people think dancing keeps the world in balance."

Naty says, "Today I get to dance in the parade. And I've got new boots, too."

"When I was a boy, I was a cactus in the parade," Old José
tells Naty.
She frowns. "But a cactus can't dance."

The road to town is busy and bouncy.

"Papa!" Naty shouts. "Look at the feather dancers! Are they coming to the fiesta?"

"Everyone's coming," says Papa.

"It's Guelaguetza, after all," says their neighbor, Old José. "People are coming from all over."

For my father, Ferucio, and his grandchildren

Author's note: Guelaguetza is a cultural festival of folkloric dances
from the seven regions of Oaxaca in southern Mexico.
It is celebrated on the last two Mondays of July.

Distributed in Canada by Douglas & McIntyre Ltd.
Color separations by Hong Kong Scanner Arts
Printed and bound in the United States of America by Berryville Graphics
First edition, 2000

Library of Congress Cataloging-in-Publication Data
Freschet, Gina.
    Naty's parade / Gina Freschet. — 1st ed.
            p.   cm.
    Summary: Naty is excited to be dancing in the fiesta parade, until she gets
lost in the city streets and cannot find the parade again.
        ISBN 0-374-35500-2
        [1. Parades—Fiction. 2. Festivals—Fiction. 3. Lost children—Fiction.] I. Title.
PZ7.F889685Nat   2000
[E]—dc21   98-52307

Naty's Parade

Gina Freschet

Farrar Straus Giroux • New York